Let's Go Out

First published in 2010
by Wayland

This paperback edition published in 2011 by Wayland

Wayland
338 Euston Road
London NW1 3BH

Wayland Australia
Level 17/207 Kent Street
Sydney, NSW 2000

Series Editor: Louise John
Editor: Katie Powell
Cover design: Paul Cherrill
Design: D.R.ink
Consultant: Shirley Bickler

A CIP catalogue record for this book is available from the British Library.

ISBN 9780750260428 (hbk)
ISBN 9780750260466 (pbk)

Printed in China

Wayland is a division of Hachette Children's Books,
an Hachette UK Company

www.hachette.co.uk

Let's Go Out

Written by Annemarie Young
Illustrated by Louise Redshaw

WAYLAND

I put on my T-shirt.

I put on my socks.

I put on my jumper.

9

I put on my coat.

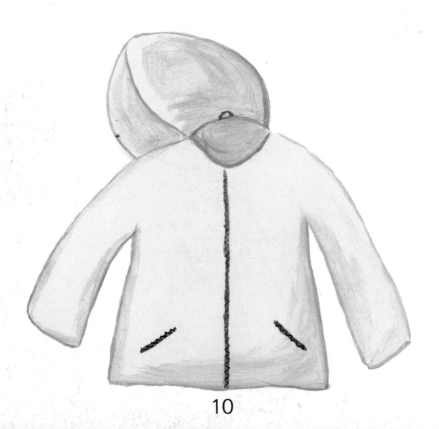

11

I put on my scarf.

I put on my gloves.

I put on my hat.

I put on my boots.

Let's go out!

Guiding a First Read of
Let's Go Out

It is important to talk through the book with the child before they read it alone. This prepares them for the way the story unfolds, and allows them to enjoy the pictures as you both talk naturally, using the language they will later encounter when reading. Read the brief overview below, and then follow the suggestions:

1. Talking through the book
The boy was getting ready to go outside to play. He tells us about the clothes he put on.

Let's read the title: **Let's Go Out!**
What item of clothing did the boy put on first?
Turn to page 4. He said, "I put on my T-shirt."
Let's look at page 6. What did he say here?
On page 8 he got a jumper. So what did he say?
Yes, "I put on my jumper."

Continue through the book, guiding the discussion to fit the text as the child looks at the illustrations.

On page 18, what does he put on last?
Yes, his boots! Turn over to the final page, and the family are ready to go outside. They all say, "Let's go out!"

2. A first reading of the book

Ask the child to read the book independently, pointing carefully under each word (tracking), while thinking about the story. Praise attempts by the child to correct themselves, and prompt them to use their letter knowledge, the punctuation and check the meaning, for example:

> **You said, "I put on my jacket." It does look like a jacket. What sound does 'jacket' start with? Yes, 'j'.**
>
> **Now try it again and see if 'jacket' is right. What else could it be? Well done, it is 'c' for 'coat'.**

3. Follow-up activities

The high frequency words in this title are:

I   my   on   put

- Select a new high frequency word, and ask the child or group to find it throughout the book. Discuss the shape of the letters and the letter sounds.
- To memorise the word, ask the child to write it in the air, then write it repeatedly on a whiteboard or on paper, leaving a space between each attempt.

4. Encourage

- Reading the book again – with expression.
- Drawing a picture based on the story.
- Writing one or two sentences using the practised word.

START READING is a series of highly enjoyable books for beginner readers. **The books have been carefully graded to match the Book Bands widely used in schools.** This enables readers to be sure they choose books that match their own reading ability.

Look out for the Band colour on the book in our Start Reading logo.

The Bands are:

| Pink Band 1A & 1B |
| Red Band 2 |
| Yellow Band 3 |
| Blue Band 4 |
| Green Band 5 |
| Orange Band 6 |
| Turquoise Band 7 |
| Purple Band 8 |
| Gold Band 9 |

START READING books can be read independently or shared with an adult. They promote the enjoyment of reading through satisfying stories supported by fun illustrations.

Annemarie Young lives in Cambridge but grew up in a city by the sea. She and her family like going for walks whatever the weather, building sand castles and finding all sorts of bugs in the garden.

Louise Redshaw likes to go for long walks and eat picnic lunches with friends when she's not too busy drawing. She loves animals but likes donkeys the most and one day wants to have a huge garden where she can keep her own donkey.